I0728529

THE CRESCENT MOON

David Neth

The Crescent Moon

Batavia, NY

www.davidnethbooks.com

Publisher: David Neth
Copyediting: Tammy Salyer of Inspired Ink Editing
Proofreading: John Ognibene
Cover Design: kpgs.designs@gmail.com

ISBN: 978-1-945336-96-6

First edition

Subscribe to the author's newsletter for updates and exclusive content:
davidnethbooks.com/newsletter

Follow the author at
www.facebook.com/davidnethbooks
www.twitter.com/davidnethbooks
www.instagram.com/dneth13

MORE BY THE AUTHOR

To find the rest of the books in the Under the Moon Series as well as
more books by the author, visit
davidnethbooks.com/books

* * *

Subscribe to his newsletter to be the first to know of new releases and
special deals!
davidnethbooks.com/newsletter

BLAZE

A Short Story

DAVID NETH

BLAZE

The sun baked down on Chris's already tanned skin. The dry heat over the dusty terrain offered no protection. Not that it mattered to him. He was used to high temperatures.

His wavy red hair had grown long and covered his neck. It blew in the gentle breeze. Sweat collected underneath his growing beard. His appearance had changed dramatically since he'd left Erie. As had he.

Chris wasn't sure exactly where he was. Somewhere in the Pacific Northwest was all he knew. It had been two years since his life had crumbled. Just as long as his bliss had lasted.

Two years had taken him from Erie to the Pacific Ocean, and now he was working his way back to the East Coast. Two years and he still hadn't found the sorcerer who killed his daughter; who tore apart his marriage. He vowed to search everywhere for "Q," as Chris knew him. Q hadn't been the one who ordered the attack, but he was the murderer. Both he and whoever put the mark on Chris's daughter were hard to track.

The night before, Chris had been at a bar in Mountain Home, Idaho, where several magical customers were regulars. They were known throughout the area—not that there were a lot of people in the area. Chris had been meeting with a wizard who had allegedly last seen Q a few months ago. A stretch, but the best thing Chris had at the moment. A lot could happen in "a few months."

"No one has seen Q," the old man, Jerry, had said the night before. Despite the heat, he'd worn a denim jacket and long pants and boots. He'd had a black bandana on his head to collect his sweat. Chris was used to these types of guys. The ones who acted rough around the edges but had never been on the opposite end of a punch.

Jerry had taken a sip of his beer and wiped his mouth with the back of his hand. He leaned in close to Chris, who tried not to turn his face when the smell of beer came wafting from Jerry's breath. "It's like she damn near fell off the face of the earth. Used to hang out down by the highway stop and prey on stupid folk."

"Yeah?" Chris took a sip of his own drink. So Q was a woman. That was a useful piece of information. But not the reason he was there.

Jerry let out a throaty laugh, still too close for Chris's comfort. "Used to tell little kids that she'd grant their wishes. Parents started to think she was a pervert. Or some kind of sadistic kidnapper who would be the focus of a *20/20* special in the future. I'm sure the cops were called. So she hightailed it out of there."

"Was that the last place you saw her?"

Jerry leaned back and reached for his drink. "I never said that."

Chris let out a huff of air. Jerry was wasting his time, probably hoping to get another free drink out of him. "So what are you saying? What can you tell me about where Q might be now?"

"What's the rush, kiddo? Chasing trouble is just plain stupid."

Kiddo.

The word had tested Chris's patience more than Jerry already was. Nothing made him feel more discredited than being referred to as a kid. That was part of the reason he grew the beard. That, and it protected his face from the sun.

Chris rubbed his beard absently. "Okay. It's obvious Q isn't here anymore, so I'll tell you what: I'll buy your next two drinks if you tell me where Q is heading."

Jerry flashed a yellow smile. "Since when did you become my date?"

Chris stood and grabbed him by the lapels. "I'm not messing around here! Tell me where the hell she went!"

Jerry's eyes widened. Besides the overhead country music playing, the bar was silent and Chris could feel the number of people staring. He briefly closed his eyes, letting out a sigh, and let Jerry go. He sunk back into his seat.

Fixing his shirt, Jerry nodded. "Okay. Yeah. Um…last I

knew, Q had moved on from kids and was heading east. Said she needed to take a break from the West Coast for now."

East.

Chris hoped she was heading toward Miami, or even New York City. As long as she stayed away from Erie. He couldn't return home. Nor did he want that bitch anywhere near his family again. What was left of them, at least.

Chris nodded and stood as he pulled a couple of bills out of his pocket and set them on the bar. Jerry had told him all he knew, and frankly, the talk of children was getting to him. If Sophia had never been killed, would Holly have stayed with him? How many kids would they have by now? What would his little girl look like if she had never died?

Before he had a chance to leave, Jerry grabbed his arm and said, "Hey, listen: you be careful asking around about people like this. Word spreads pretty quickly. Even here in the middle of nowhere. Hell, especially in the middle of nowhere. Now, my lips are sealed, but not everybody's will be."

Chris turned to leave, but Jerry squeezed his arm harder. "Why don't you just forget about whatever mission you're on and go home?"

Now Chris leaned in too close for Jerry's comfort.

"I can never go home."

After that, Chris had stayed the night at a roach motel in town. As long as it had air-conditioning, it was a luxury. The next morning, he set out east along the railroad tracks toward the next town, hoping to find some trace of Q. He knew it was a long shot. Whoever she was, she knew what she was doing. She knew not to leave any tracks behind. If she did, it was likely because she knew Chris was following her and she *wanted* to be tracked.

But nothing had turned up yet. The only things he knew about her were magical: a sorcerer with a persuasion specialty. He didn't know what she looked like or even her real name. Everyone who had claimed to have seen her had contradicting opinions on what she looked like. Maybe she was a shapeshifter too?

It didn't matter. He was bound and determined to find her, and he would go down swinging if it came to it. She had taken everything from him, and he intended to do the same to her. If she knew he was following her, he'd just have to be more careful.

Chris approached a little hamlet as the sun began to set. From what he could guess from the last time he looked at a map, this was Hammett. His stomach ached with hunger. He hadn't eaten anything since dinner the night before. Life on the road sometimes meant skipping meals. Lots of them. When he could, he would eat big meals to compensate. But sometimes he would go days living off of convenience store lunch snacks. His energy reflected it, too.

Hammett offered nothing in the way of restaurants—Chris would've killed for a warm meal. So he settled on prepackaged sandwiches and bottled water from the trading post on Main Street.

Once his cash had run out, Chris had become pretty good

at stealing things. He rarely used magic to assist him. That was an unfair advantage. What he was doing was still unfair, but he was desperate. Luckily, there was only one clerk at the trading post. He slipped a few snacks into his bag and then paid for the bottled water so he didn't raise suspicion.

He used to use credit cards—he had several under various aliases—but he stopped after one card was denied. He had been nearly caught by the police, but he'd managed to get away. Luckily, the card that had been flagged was for Howard Stars. If Chris ever decided to settle down anywhere, credit card fraud would be the end of him. He couldn't take that chance. He needed to keep his options open.

He wandered through town looking for a place to stay. Although a sign right outside of the trading post advertised a motel "with a TV," the place had apparently been closed for a long time. Instead, he continued wandering, looking for an abandoned house or store that he could bunk in for the night.

It was difficult in a town like this to find anywhere to stay. Some places looked abandoned but were simply unkempt. Eventually, he came across a trailer that apparently belonged to a trucker who was currently on the road. The yard mostly consisted of a long wraparound driveway that made parking a truck easier. The house itself was likely smaller than the trailer the trucker usually pulled.

It didn't take long for Chris to find the key and let himself in. Most people hid a spare in the same usual spots: under the welcome mat, in a piece of decoration, or on a ledge above the door. This one had been inside the gutter, which threatened to rip free of the house at any minute.

As soon as Chris stepped in, he was hit with the strong smell of mildew. Somewhere, there was a leak from the last time it had rained. Apparently, not since the trucker had last been home.

After opening a window, Chris took a look around. It wasn't the worst place he had stayed—certainly better than the night before—but each night he was still reminded of the life he used to lead. Lying down in a comfortable bed after a long day of work next to a beautiful wife while their daughter slept in the next room.

Taking a deep breath, Chris stomped those thoughts out. That wasn't his life anymore and it was never going to be again.

He took a seat on the couch and tested how comfortable it would be to sleep on. The cushions were plump, but when he leaned back he felt moisture. He found the leak. The frame that held the window above the couch was rotted, and Chris thought that if he tried to open the window, it just might fall out.

Groaning, he went down the narrow hallway to the bedroom. He usually tried to stay out of people's bedrooms. He didn't like to invade their privacy. Sure, he was squatting, but usually only for one night. He had every intention of locking up and returning the key where he'd found it the next day. Make it look like he was never there.

Still, there were times he needed to steal some things to get by. Twenty bucks, a hoodie, something to eat. He always had a reason to justify stealing: fast cash, something to wear in the rain, or just plain survival.

The bedroom at the end of the hall was small and messy. The sheets were stained and Chris couldn't imagine sleeping there. Occasionally, if the place was nice and seemed clean, he would sleep in a bed, but usually he opted for the couch. Tonight it looked like he was getting the floor, though. It was still better than some places he had slept.

Before he left the bedroom, he raided the man's dresser. Chris hadn't had access to a washing machine in over a week, and his short supply of clothes all stank of sweat. Unfortunately, the man who lived there seemed to be much larger than Chris—not that that was difficult with the way Chris ate nowadays. Still, he pulled a few clean T-shirts from the dresser and stuffed them in his bag.

The best thing about this part of the country was that the lack of trees or buildings meant the sun seemed to take longer to set. That left Chris enough time to shower and hand-wash his clothes in the bathroom sink. He didn't dare turn on a light. Once the sunlight was gone, he did what he could in the dark, but usually he went to bed. It allowed him to get up early the next day and sneak out before the rest of the town woke up and saw him leaving whatever placed he'd camped out for the night.

Chris emerged from the bathroom in the large white T-shirt he'd just stolen. He was towel-drying his hair when a bright light blinded him for a moment before it faded. A woman stood in the middle of the small living room after the light subsided.

"You have been very hard to find." She wore blue robes with

a single upside-down triangle on the front—the standard uniform for a member of the Fire Wizards.

Chris shrugged. "That's because I don't want to be found." He took a seat on the arm of the wet couch and ignored the dampness. "What do you want?" He folded his arms across his chest. He was vulnerable if she attacked, but he was too defiant at the moment.

"My name is Raven, I'm a member—"

"I know who you are. I asked you what you want."

She sighed. Chris could tell she didn't like being interrupted. "There has been talk about an unknown power being released. Something called the Chaos. As a coven, we believe that it will equip one person with more power than any one person should have—more than any one person can defeat."

"A couple of things," Chris counted on each of his fingers, "who has been talking? Why come to me? And why do you care?" He had previously been targeted by the Fire Wizards—some would even call it *chased*—but they'd never asked him for help before.

She rolled her eyes but tried to maintain her composure when she spoke. "The leaders of the Fire Wizards have heard from several sources about a group who is looking to release the Chaos and have taken quite a few steps to achieving that. We care because it could be the end of our coven and yours, too."

"I don't have a coven," Chris said.

"So join ours. Better yet, lead it."

"What?"

"You heard me. In the last few years, the leaders have gotten older. More careful. Too cautious, in my opinion. I'm not alone in thinking that we need someone with conviction and strength. You, Mr. Harper, fit the bill."

"I've already told you, no."

The Fire Wizards had been following him for a long time now. As much as he kept moving to find Q, he was also moving to get away from the Fire Wizards. They were the reason Sophia was dead. They were the ones who had her killed. From day one, his answer had been no different. The fact that they now wanted him to lead didn't change that. "Get out."

Raven began to open her mouth to protest, but Chris shouted, "Go!" Flames trickled out of his hands as he shouted, sparking a fire on the carpet. He could've easily stomped it out, but he held his gaze on Raven instead.

Her head turned. "You're still a naïve little boy, aren't you? The two years since you burned your daughter to death has only made you more reckless."

Chris extended both of his hands to the wizard, palms out, and shot flame at her. She stumbled backward but remained on her feet. Her face was flushed from the heat when the attack stopped, but the curtains behind her had caught fire, filling the small trailer with smoke.

"This is exactly the kind of reaction you had when you killed your daughter," she spat.

"I didn't kill her!" Chris charged at her, but the smoke was thickening as the wallpaper began to catch, and she slipped out of his grasp. "You did!"

He searched through the smoke for her but could barely make out the features from across the room. His eyes watered and he pinched them with one hand while he felt around with the other.

"If you join the Fire Wizards, we could teach you how to withstand the smoke," Raven said from behind him. He whipped around, shooting his power out of his hand like a flamethrower and igniting more of the trailer. "And flame," she added just as he was struck in the side from her attack. It ignited his T-shirt.

Dropping to the floor, he patted out the fire on his shirt and winced as he pulled a piece of the charred fabric from his burnt skin. He watched as Raven's footsteps led her out the door, which helped clear some of the smoke, but the flames rose higher as fresh air entered the trailer.

Forcing himself up, Chris ran out the door before remembering his bag. He reentered long enough to snatch it up and run as far as he could from the house. A crowd was forming, and he could hear sirens in the distance. As he moved, his bag bounced on his back, slamming against his fresh burns.

Raven was nowhere in sight. With the attention the fire was drawing, she wouldn't stick around. So Chris ran as fast as he could in the direction with the fewest number of people. This had not been the first time he had made a scene with his magic, but this was the first time he had nowhere to hide. The open landscape that allowed him to work later into the night didn't offer any hiding spots.

Someone shouted from the group of onlookers, "Hey, grab

him!" A few people moved toward Chris, but nobody came close to stopping him. His side ached from the burn, which only intensified as sweat dripped down his skin. Although the oversized white T-shirt he wore was stained from the smoke, it made him stand out in the darkness.

Eventually, he recognized where he was and followed the road to the railroad tracks he'd taken into town. He ran alongside the tracks in the opposite direction from where he'd come. His feet slipped occasionally on the large stones, but he was able to regain his balance and keep running. He didn't dare slow down. Not yet.

Chris ran until he heard the rush of water from the Snake River nearby. Slowing to a walk, he lifted his arms over his head and caught his breath. When his chest was no longer burning and his breath no longer ragged, he stepped through the weeds toward the water.

After pulling off his backpack, he yanked off what was left of the white T-shirt and cringed. The burn still ached, and his sweat only made it sting worse.

Stepping into the river, Chris first tried scooping water onto the wound, but the pressure from the trickle of water made him scream out in pain. The water was up to his knees, and he was cautious of stepping deeper into the river. Without the sun, he couldn't see the bottom.

Instead, he set his few belongings to the side—most of his clothes were still hanging to dry back at the trailer—and sat in the water. He didn't want to waste any time to strip further or take the chance of somebody catching him and not being able to make a quick getaway.

The water was cold, and tears pooled in his eyes as he sank deeper into it and covered the burn. After a moment, relief washed over him. He needed to clean up again after the run anyway.

It was a new moon, and the sky was filled with stars. The longer Chris sat out there, the more he could see.

Holly would love it.

Every summer, they used to pick a night to lay out under the stars during a new moon and try to see as many as they could. Even though they went out to Presque Isle, the light from the city never allowed them to see as many as he saw now. He wished she were with him. He wondered if she ever thought about him and the happiness they had before Sophia had died. The last time he had seen Holly was the night it had happened. The heartbreak in her eyes was something Chris wanted to forget but knew he never would.

After that day, he'd isolated himself in his aunt's house long enough for the divorce papers to come in the mail. He'd known things were over between them, but he hadn't been sure if Holly would take legal actions to end their marriage.

The papers showed just how much she hated him. Worse, it showed that she blamed him for Sophia's death. She never knew the truth because she hadn't stuck around long enough to hear him out. He never confronted her because he knew he'd see that same anguished look on her face. That would shatter him to pieces.

So he set himself on a mission: find whoever killed Sophia and get justice for her death. Even if it would never put his family back together, he needed to do that for his daughter.

* * *

Chris woke up a couple of hours later. The sun hadn't risen yet and he had slumped into the water further. It now was up past his shoulders. Pulling himself from his resting spot, he used the charred T-shirt as a towel. Even though he was only dabbing at his side, his skin was still too irritated for any contact.

He pulled on a fresh T-shirt and slung his backpack over his shoulder. Despite the pain, he would have to keep it covered once the sun rose. It was best to move while it was still dark.

He didn't want to look at the burn marks. He could feel that they were inflamed. The water had helped, but it wasn't a miracle cure. Back when he had still lived at home, Josh could've whipped up an ointment or something to help him heal faster. He hadn't talked to his brother in over a year when he'd decided to dump his cell phone so he could no longer be tracked.

The early morning sky provided no light for Chris to guide himself along the uneven terrain of the tracks. He could see the sun rising in the distance, but the light still hadn't reached him yet. He tried to keep his focus on his feet and carry on. It had been a while since he'd last looked at a map this far east, so he was hoping the tracks would lead to another town. Preferably somewhere that could offer a place to eat—his stomach was aching again—and a better place to sleep. All he wanted to do was take an ice bath and lick his wounds for a bit, but he figured it might be a while before he would be able to do that.

As he walked, he thought of Raven's attack. It bothered him. The Fire Wizards had given up trying to get him to join them, so why attack him again? The last few times had been arguments with the threat of magical interference, but this time she had seemed to be taunting him to attack. Was it a test? She said they had been watching him—which came as no surprise to him—but did she want to experience the extent of his magic firsthand? If so, why?

Was Raven serious about wanting him to lead? Could he? Why would she think he would even consider it? Did she think he was that desperate? Was he?

Even more confusing was the business about the Chaos. Did such a thing exist? Why did she think that Chris—a loner witch with no magic book and no coven—would be able to defeat something so powerful? If he was being honest, he no longer cared what happened to other people. Magic had robbed him of so much already that he knew he was playing a losing game by trying to save people. When he was younger, he, Josh, and Holly had been so stupid to think that they could make a difference in people's lives. They were just three teenaged witches. What could they do to change the inevitable outcome?

The railroad tracks led Chris to another small town. Trash cans and garbage bags were out along the residential streets.

Garbage day.

Chris smiled. It wasn't the best conditions, but with any luck, he could find something to fill his stomach. Previously, he had found stale cereal or leftovers from fruit to nibble on. He was at least hoping for some stale bread or expired Pop-Tarts.

Only once he had gotten sick—the mold on an apple apparently went further than Chris wanted to admit. At the time, he was afraid he was going to have to go to the hospital, but eventually he got better. It taught him to be more careful when resorting to Dumpster diving.

Unhitching the bear-proof trash cans, Chris smiled when he spotted a full box of club crackers, still sealed. The expiration date was from the year before, but it didn't matter to him. He tucked it under his arm and tried to tidy up the bag to cover his tracks.

The sky was brightening. He needed to get someplace safe so nobody would call him out for going through their trash. The less attention, the better. Especially now.

Staying out of the sun was essential to his recovery. So was water, which he was certainly lacking. He didn't even think about asking for help. His lack of ID would raise suspicions if he passed out and ended up at a hospital.

Chris found a spot under a tree next to the river. Pulling out his lucky find, he tried to brush off as much of the salt from the crackers as he could. He needed to keep his body hydrated, and the salt wasn't going to do him any good.

After he was done eating, he considered his options. He tried to recall the names of the towns from when he first traveled to the West Coast. If he remembered correctly, he was now in Glenns Ferry or King Hill. The next large city—and his closest bet to get medical attention—was Twin Falls. That was too far of a walk for him in his condition. He could backtrack to Mountain Home, but he didn't want to lose any time. Q was heading east, and he intended to be on her toes. As much as he could, at least. His injury already forced him to wait until sunset to leave the shelter of the shade.

Besides, getting professional medical attention was out of the question. They would be too curious, and he needed a quick recovery. Despite a few questionable moments, he hadn't needed anyone's help yet. Not that anyone else was around to prove anything to. Still, the idea of going to a hospital seemed like the cowardly way out. He had taken care of himself just fine up until this point. He didn't need anyone.

Staying put wouldn't help him, either. Eventually, the search for the arsonist would spread to the towns surrounding Hammett and they would find him. It was nearly impossible to hide in a small town.

Out of options, Chris made up his mind. He wasn't happy about it, but he figured he might be able to make it benefit him in the end. For the time being, though, he needed to heal. Treating his burns with warm, dirty river water was only going to lead to infection and other problems for him sooner than later.

Still, he spent the rest of the day under a tree near the river. Once the sun had moved and cast a portion of the river in the shade, he slipped into the water for relief. All day, he wanted to sleep off the pain, but he couldn't get comfortable. No matter how he lay, he irritated something.

Chris remembered when his specialty had first expanded. He'd been so happy that he could finally yield flame. Of course, that had also meant he needed to be more careful. Especially once Sophia had come along. And he thought he was, until…

Using the tree to lift himself out of the water, he cringed as his body protested against his movement. His stomach churned. He needed to eat again. And he needed water. Desperately.

He hadn't had anything to drink all day, and he was feeling it. Dry-mouthed and fatigued, he wandered through town until he found the railroad tracks again and followed them east. He walked for what felt like an hour, although he figured his dehydration warped his sense of time. The sun had mostly set, too, which confused him further.

For the most part, the tracks followed the Snake River. At one of the turns, the tracks turned away from any roads and houses. Although he wasn't covered by trees or anything else to offer him invisibility, he closed his eyes and prepared the spell he had been crafting all day.

It was similar to the one his wife—*ex*-wife—had written in their magic book. Something she'd used to call a member of the Fire Wizards when she'd first learned she was a witch. She had transcribed it to their magic book. He remembered what he could and filled in the parts he couldn't. In the end, any summoning spell would have worked because the Fire Wizards had been the most prevalent thing on his mind all day.

The Crescent Moon

Calling all across the skies,
your power you cannot hide.
I summon you to this space,
so I can claim my rightful place.

Raven appeared in a swirl of blue flames, momentarily casting light into the darkness. "I'm surprised you summoned me."

Chris sat on the ground. He was still shirtless from his swim in the river, and the faint breeze was a mix of pain and relief on his skin. "First thing's first: I need you to get me some water." His voice didn't sound like his own. Too dry. His tongue stuck to the roof of his mouth when he spoke.

Raven's eyes narrowed. "Why can't you get it yourself? You are a witch."

"I don't have any money, and I want to keep my use of magic to a minimum." What he really needed was to figure out how exactly to start the conversation. Although he had had all day to think about it, he mostly kept reciting the spell in his head so he wouldn't forget it. Besides, Raven had put him in this condition, she was going to help him heal. It was the first step in testing whether she could actually view him as a leader. Her leader.

She huffed and a flash of flame made Chris divert his eyes from the brightness. When he looked back, she was gone. Two minutes later, she reappeared and tossed two bottles of water at him. He guzzled the first and saved the second for later.

Clarity washed over him. He would never again underestimate the power of water. Just one bottle made him feel so much better.

Raven crossed her arms. "What do you want?"

He shrugged. "What do you think I want?"

"I don't know. You made it pretty clear yesterday that you had no interest in my offer."

"You mean when you attacked me and nearly got me arrested!?"

She waved her hand. "Details. Look, I have somewhere to be, so if you have nothing useful to say, I'm going to leave."

Chris couldn't stand the idea of being left alone in the middle of nowhere. If he continued at this rate, he would be dead by the end of the week. The burn had swelled more than he cared to admit. The dirty water was likely giving him an infection, just as he'd feared.

"I'll do it!" he shouted as the flames began to swirl around Raven.

She stopped her magic and smiled. "Did I chew you down?"

"You're awfully smug to someone who is about to be your boss."

"That arrangement still has yet to be worked out."

He cocked an eyebrow. "What? I thought your whole point for attacking me yesterday was to get me to lead you?"

"See it from our side: you've been turning us down for some time now. We can't believe your loyalty would shift this quickly."

"So why is the offer even still good?" Chris didn't see how this added up. For years he had been under the impression that the Fire Wizards were running out of members with true power.

Now, all of a sudden, they thought they held the cards.

"You have potential and we don't want to lose that potential," she said. "Still, we have to be sure that you're not going to betray us. You'll be under surveillance for some time until we can be certain that you're one of us."

"So I'm going to be on probation?"

She nodded. "Of sorts, yes."

"What's wrong with someone who has already shown their loyalty? Someone already a part of your coven?"

For a moment, Chris's thoughts went to Drew, who had been a member of the Fire Wizards prior to meeting Chris and his brother. He wondered if Drew would have been targeted to lead if he were still alive. Chris still couldn't get the image of Drew's bloody corpse from his mind. Another thing Holly probably held against him.

"We've been looking, but so far no one has shown the strength in their abilities like you," she explained.

"So why should I follow along with your probation? Couldn't I just take out whoever questions my authority?" He had no intention of doing that, but he needed to show that he couldn't be walked on. He needed their help healing, but he didn't know what he would do once he was better.

"I said you have potential. You still have a lot to learn. As we teach you, we'll assess your loyalty." She motioned to his side. "The first thing we'll do, though, is address those burns. Each and every one of us has been in the same pain you're experiencing now. Protecting yourself against the flame will be your first lesson."

That was good news. She offered and he didn't have to ask. "But I'm not a wizard."

"The only thing that sets wizards apart from witches is the use of a wand. Spells, charms, potions, incantations—everything we use can be used by both witches and wizards." She stepped closer and stuck out her hand. "Do we have a deal?"

Chris studied her a moment. He had no other options. Right now, he needed a safe place to go to rest and recover. Maybe the Fire Wizards even had advanced treatments that they would give him? He had never noticed any burn scars on any of the Fire Wizards he'd come in contact with yet. What did she really have in store for him?

Once he could prove his loyalty, he would be in the perfect position to use the Fire Wizards to help him find Q. The sheer number of them would make a world of difference. Maybe once he had avenged his daughter's death, he could focus his attention on restoring the Fire Wizards to their previous mission: protecting the nonmagical. After their brief conversion to the dark side, they'd never seemed to go back to the way they had been before. Now, they were neither good nor evil. They had their own agenda, and Chris was curious to figure out what that was.

Still, he had his own agenda to keep too, and this was an opportunity for him. He had to take it.

Grasping Raven's hand and pulling himself up to a standing position, he said, "On one condition."

She shook her head. "You're not in the position to be—"

"My family is off-limits."

He knew he had hurt them by leaving. And he knew he would hurt them again once they found out he was not only a member of the Fire Wizards, but leading them. He didn't want to ever physically hurt them. They had been through enough. Especially Holly.

"Everyone—my brother, my aunt, my wife—"

"Ex-wife," Raven corrected.

Chris squeezed her hand so her knuckles ground together. "Anyone who becomes a future member of my family is off-limits too. Got it?"

Raven stared at Chris for a moment. "I think your family's immunity can be arranged. Welcome aboard, Mr. Harper."

TIMEOUT

A Short Story

DAVID NETH

TIMEOUT

As you all know by now, *Spellbinding* is a special book for me and I think this rollout is a great way to emphasize that to my readers." Kathy flipped back to the first page of her marketing packet and gave Greg a sideways smile. He had been her editor since *Possessed* had first been picked up. He had helped her restructure her first novel to make sense out of it, finding the story that all the other publishers had failed to see. Now, almost five years later, he was still working with her.

"Well, we're very excited to continue working with you, Kathy," Paul, the publisher of DJ Books, said. It was a small publishing company, but Kathy's first two books had been picking up steam on the charts after her appearance on a satellite radio show kicked up some sales. They had additional income to put toward marketing *Spellbinding.*

"Two more months, and then this will be out for everyone to see. Are you excited?" Paul asked.

Kathy beamed. "Are you kidding? Yeah!" This marketing plan was a lot more high-profile than she—or DJ Books—had ever implemented before. Every ounce of excitement was also met with the same amount of apprehension. What if the book wasn't as good as her previous two? What if with each new appearance she just humiliated herself?

She pushed those doubts away. Here was a whole team of people who all thought the book deserved the rollout it was getting. They helped make the book great. Besides, they had had her back with the last two books. This one wouldn't be any different.

"Well, good luck at your photo shoot this weekend. I'm sure they'll turn out great."

Kathy smiled and thanked them before leaving.

The photo shoot was new. Something to signify her prominence as an author. She had never had a professional author photo done before. The website DJ Books set up for her featured the photos taken by newspapers and other literary magazines. She was both excited and nervous about how they would turn out.

At the elevator, Greg called her name and she held the door for him.

"Thanks." He leaned against the railing. "They're really excited. You're the best-selling author of this company. Seriously, I don't know if I would even still have a job if they hadn't picked up your first book."

Kathy smiled. "You and me both." After ten years at the *Erie Review*, she was finally putting in her two weeks' notice. The success of her second book had led to more sales of her first book, and now she had a padded bank account and needed more time to write. And promote.

Silence filled the elevator as they descended to the ground floor. Kathy didn't know much about Greg. Sure, she had spent several hours over the course of three books on the phone with him, but they discussed plot lines, character development, and word choices. Nothing personal. The elevator seemed to slow as the silence grew louder.

"So, uh, what are you working on now that you've finished this series?" Greg asked.

Kathy readjusted her purse on her shoulder. "Well, I've got a few ideas. I'm halfway through a romance manuscript, but I'm not sure it's going to go anywhere. Definitely not something DJ Books typically publishes."

Greg shrugged. "I bet it's great. I'd love to take a look at it sometime."

The elevator dinged and the doors opened.

"I don't know if it's ready for anyone else's eyes but mine just yet." She stepped out and he trailed behind.

Greg put up his hands. "Hey, I get it. You're an artist. You decide when your masterpiece is ready for consumption."

Kathy laughed as she pushed on the outside door leading to the busy New York City sidewalk. "Yeah, and once I hand it over, you can tear it apart."

They stopped outside. Kathy wanted to head to the train station and find a good book that she could read on the ride back to Erie, but she could tell that Greg had something else to say, so she held off her good-bye.

"Would you like to get some drinks with me?"

Kathy looked down at the ground for a moment and brushed her hair out of her eyes. "Greg, I'm not sure…"

She didn't know what to say. Greg was a great guy, someone she could possibly call a friend—if she knew anything about his personal life—but she had no interest in dating him. She had no interest in dating anyone at the moment. But she hated to see the look of disappointment creeping across his face. "I'm not sure I'll have enough time today," she finally said.

He smiled. "Just one quick drink, I promise. I know this place two blocks over. They have the best martinis there."

Kathy nodded and followed him.

The bar was a hole-in-the-wall, as most places of the kind were in New York. But it was still early afternoon, so it was quiet. They got a table and ordered.

Kathy flattened out the cocktail napkin in front of her. "Besides the romance, I've been thinking about this other book. One about a shapeshifter, but not necessarily a witch. Maybe there's an accident or something that gives him his powers and he does cool stuff with it."

"Sounds thrilling."

Kathy smiled. "Obviously, I have a few details to work out."

"More like you have the whole book to work out."

"Whatever! Like you have a bunch of great ideas yourself."

He held up a finger. "Actually, I've done a few work-for-hires. Under a pen name, but yes, I do have some ideas."

"Really?" Kathy was surprised. Greg had a lot of great suggestions—and he could certainly write—but she didn't think he even *wanted* to write a book.

He nodded.

"Anything I know?"

"Oh. No. Nothing you'd want to read. It's stupid."

"No, tell me!"

He bowed his head and scratched it. "Um…well, it was back when *Twilight* was huge, so I wrote a vampire…romance. Let's call it romance."

"It was smut, wasn't it?" Kathy tried to stifle her giggles.

In reply, he turned his hands, palms up.

Kathy covered her mouth with her hands and laughed. Greg Martin, who never seemed to run out of plaid shirts and khakis to wear to work, was the author of a teen smut novel. She couldn't believe it.

"I actually asked you out for a different reason. I mean, I wanted to get to know you on a personal level—as a friend!" He didn't meet her eyes, and his hands couldn't find a comfortable resting spot. "I mean, we've been working together for almost five years and I don't know much about you."

She grew serious. In hindsight, laughing was rude. Especially when it was so painfully obvious that Greg had other intentions for this outing.

The bartender brought over their drinks, which allowed Kathy time to think of a more eloquent response. "Well, I have two nephews. They're older now—adults, rather. Josh is a doctor back in Erie—well, he's doing his residency, but almost. And my other nephew…" She bit her bottom lip. "He, uh, he's been traveling a lot."

Greg smiled and played with the bottom of his martini glass for a moment before standing and leaning in toward Kathy. She backed away and turned. His kiss landed on her ear.

He stepped back and ran his hands over his head. "Sorry! I'm sorry! I shouldn't have done that. That was crossing a line."

"No, Greg, it's okay. Just sit back down," she urged.

He pulled out a few bills from his wallet and laid them on the table. "No, I should go. We have a professional relationship that works. We need to keep it at that."

"I'm divorced!" Kathy blurted.

Her words reverberated throughout the empty bar and her cheeks flushed. More importantly, it stopped him in his tracks, and he finally met her eyes. "What? What does that have to do— was it recently?"

She shook her head. "No. A little over ten years ago."

"I'm sorry. I, uh—I'm having a hard time finding the relevance here."

Kathy motioned to his chair. "Just sit." He took a seat. "My whole relationship with my, uh, husband was…tumultuous, I suppose. Up and down with the emotions. I went from being the happiest I've ever been to the most depressed I've ever been over and over. It was hard."

"I'm sorry, Kathy. I didn't know. But that was so long ago. If you don't mind me asking, why does it still bother you? You've moved on, right?"

"Um…not entirely. After we first split up, he kept trying to win me back, and I kept pushing him further and further away, and I really just shut off that part of my life, you know? Where you want to share everything with one person and you trust them completely." She shrugged. "I thought I could trust him, and I couldn't." Her eyes welled up as she thought of her sister. "And now, I don't think that I should even bother."

She dabbed at her eyes with the cocktail napkin. "Sorry. I wasn't expecting to lay that all out there, but I just needed to explain to you that I'm not rejecting you, but the whole thing."

"Don't say that—"

"I've had my time and it didn't work out. I'm not saying everyone's like that, but I don't want to go through that again. I just want to focus on something I can control. Like my career."

"C'mon, you can't be serious. You're a beautiful, intelligent, successful wo—"

"Stop trying to cheer me up. Please. I didn't unload this on you for pity. I just wanted you to understand." She zipped up her purse and stood. "Now I have to go. I don't want to miss my train. Thank you for the drink. I'll let you know when I've finished my next manuscript."

As she walked past him, he reached for her hand. "Kathy."

"What?"

"I would like to see you again. Outside of work. Nothing romantic or anything. You just look like you could use a friend."

She gave him a sad smile and squeezed his hand before walking out.

* * *

Train rides were always so intriguing to Kathy. Sure, she could teleport anywhere, but her life had become so busy—she always seemed like she was in rush—that it was nice to just sit for several hours on a train and lose herself in a book or in her writing. It wasted a day, but she needed it. She needed a day to herself to unwind and relax and not think about anything.

Whenever she had a meeting with her publisher, she looked forward to riding the train in and out. At this moment, however, she wished that she hadn't already purchased a train ticket. She was making money from writing, sure, but she was not rich by anyone's standards. She just wanted to be home alone away from crowds.

Kathy walked swiftly to the train station. How could she just unload that on him? Greg was a nice guy, and he had been a huge part of her career, but that was the extent of their relationship. She was humiliated. Greg would probably always think of her as the sad, broken, divorced woman who was always on the verge of a breakdown.

Crazy. That was what she was to him now.

She just hoped he didn't tell anyone. She didn't think he would, but at a small company, word traveled fast. She'd learned that at the literary magazine, and she didn't want to see the look of pity in everyone's eyes. The same look that Greg had given her.

What was worse was she didn't even realize that everything with Will still bothered her so much. He had been out of her life for ten years.

So had Samantha.

It was the loss of her sister and Kathy's own betrayal that still haunted her. Not Will. She would never be able to make it up to her. Her recklessness had cost her her sister. She couldn't put all the blame on Will for that, no matter how much she still hated him or how dead he was.

At Penn Station, she made a beeline for the bathroom. She didn't want to talk to anyone until she had a chance to compose herself.

Standing in front of the mirror, she assessed the damage. Nothing too bad. Her makeup had held up for the most part. She hadn't been full-on crying, which was good—for her ride home and Greg's image of her.

She stopped at the bookstore and browsed through a shelf of paperbacks. One of the goals she'd set for herself was to see her book everywhere—including this small bookstore in the train station. But DJ Books was still too small to make that kind of deal for her. She was successful, but she was still what the Big 5 publishers considered a "midlist author." Now that she was out of her contract with DJ Books, she would be able to consider other options.

An old man's voice carried in from the busy concourse. "The Chaos is coming! Witches beware!"

Kathy rolled her eyes and snatched a book from the shelf and got in line. Her trip to New York was not complete without a crackhead shouting conspiracy theories into the air.

As she waited, she caught sight of the man out of the corner of her eye and diverted her attention to the front display by the register. She had learned from previous experience that it was best not to make eye contact.

"The Chaos is coming! Kathy, you gotta be careful!"

Kathy's head snapped to him. How did he know her name? Then she noticed his eyes roll back into place just before he turned away from her and continued his shouts throughout the crowd.

Tossing her book on a nearby shelf, she tried to catch up to him without drawing attention to herself. The man had mixed himself in with the crowd, which traveled in all different directions. Security men and dogs were scattered throughout the station, but they didn't make a move on the man.

As he descended the escalators down to the subway, Kathy was able to grasp his arm and pull him down a side hallway. There weren't many people down this wing. Those who were there were in too much of a rush to notice her and the man.

"How do you know my name?"

"The Chaos!" he shouted.

"Stop it!" She put up her hands, and the busy train station

fell silent as they froze in place. They were the only two not affected by her magic. "I asked you a question!"

His eyes grew large as he looked at her. He slowly shook his head. "Kathy…be careful. The Chaos will be here soon!"

"What is the Chaos? What are you talking about?"

"It's coming!" His eyes rolled back in his head again, showing only the whites.

Kathy shook her head. A possession. Just as she suspected. She held the man against the wall as she thought of the dispossession spell from her magic book. It called for instruments to make the spell stronger, but she hoped that the words would be enough to release the man from the spirit's hold. There weren't any conflicting spirits that would interfere—at least, not that she could see.

For the spirit that wants to hide,
it's time for you to say good-bye.
Release this vessel from your grasp,
and return from where you were cast.

The man's eyes shone white as the spirit left his body. Kathy glanced up at their reflection in the security mirror by the ceiling and saw a glow. She looked behind her and didn't see anything. The glow was only present in the mirror. As she stepped closer, it formed a familiar shape: her sister, Samantha.

Kathy's mouth fell open. She wanted to scream and ask a thousand different questions: How was she? How did she get there? Why was she there? Had she been watching over them all along? Was her presence significant? Was she the one possessing the man? Why?

Before Kathy could even put together a coherent sentence, Samantha's spirit in the mirror faded.

A loud clap of thunder broke Kathy's mesmerized stare at the mirror. But that didn't make sense. How could she hear thunder down in the depths of Penn Station? It must've been a train.

But then she heard it again.

It was definitely not a train. She weaved through the frozen people up two flights of stairs and onto the sidewalk. It was quiet now, due to her magic. She had grown to be able to stop time completely.

The sky boomed yet again.

Kathy looked up and saw a darkening cloud covering the bright blue sky. But something was off about it. Different. It wasn't a normal storm cloud. She couldn't figure out what about it wasn't normal, though.

It wasn't until the cloud reached the sun and hid its rays from the earth that she saw what it truly was: deep purple.

As it continued to roll across the sky, Kathy watched as pieces shot to the ground. First, it was just one strand of cloud, but then more and more reached down to the earth until the cloud itself was falling.

The man next to Kathy was struck by a falling piece, and Kathy's magic immediately wore off. He fell to the ground clutching at his throat and gasping for air as the cloud filled his lungs.

"Are you okay?" Kathy knelt next to him and tried to pull his hands away from his neck.

He stopped convulsing and his body went limp. She put her ear to his mouth and listened for the sound of his breathing.

Nothing.

She lined her hands up to begin chest compressions, but his eyes flashed open. He looked at her with murderous eyes and latched his hands on to her throat.

Swatting at him, she tried to stand so she could push away from him with her legs, but her heels didn't give her much balance.

Her vision began to blur, and she gave up trying to pull his hands off. She balled up one fist and slammed it into his cheek.

He released his hold, and the sky began to clear up. Soon, Kathy's magic wore off, and the noise resumed all around her. She walked away from the man she'd punched before she could see if he was all right. He had freaked her out too much.

On her way back home, she tried to busy herself with her book, but she couldn't focus on the story. Her sister was on her mind. Instead of reading, she stared out the window and wondered what life would be like if Samantha were still alive. Would Josh still be using magic? Would Chris still be in contact with his family? Would Kathy be just as successful as she was now? Or would she never have formed the drive to succeed if her sister continued to take care of her?

None of that mattered now. Samantha wouldn't have shown herself if she didn't want to send a message. Kathy just needed to figure out what that message was. Was that purple cloud the message? She had never seen anything like it, but judging by the man's reaction, it wasn't good.

She debated if she should tell Josh about his mother's visit when she got home but decided against it. Until she knew more of the story, it was best not to stress him out any more than he already was.

Her phone buzzed and she looked and saw it was Greg. Their awkward encounter after her meeting seemed like a lifetime ago. Besides, she was not in the mood to talk about any possible relationship. She just needed to think.

All she wanted to do was reminisce about her sister. It had been a long ten years, and the only sight of Samantha had been in photographs. That had changed today. Greg wouldn't understand—he couldn't understand. To him, magic was fiction. To Kathy, magic was very much a reality. One that gave her so many abilities while also taking away so much.

Her phone rang again. This time from an unfamiliar number. Confused, she decided to answer it. If it was Greg, she would just tell him to give her some time. She would explain to him later that she wasn't crazy. Well, try to.

"Hello?"

"It's me. I need your help."

BLOWN AWAY

A Short Story

DAVID NETH

Blown Away

Mrs. Kors lay silently in her hospital bed as the monitor next to her chirped with every heartbeat. It was just a pacemaker that she had put in, but her body wasn't accepting it very well. The surgeons were forced to remove it after she'd developed an infection. Due to her allergies with different medications, it was nearly impossible to treat. The outlook didn't look good. Her heart was weakening each day.

Josh had been visiting her regularly since she'd first been admitted. Although she had always been the nosy, annoying neighbor from across the street, he now missed her intrusions. He remembered back to how persistent she had been when his mother had died. Mrs. Kors was always calling, bringing over food, or asking how he and his brother were doing in school. She had been the one who had watched them get on the bus when they'd first started school.

Now here she was at the mercy of Josh and his colleagues.

He placed one hand over Mrs. Kors's heart and another on his own. Magic was mostly foreign to him now, but he was willing to try for his elderly neighbor.

Healing power and healing words,
open your eyes. You are cured.

With a jerk, Mrs. Kors's monitor jumped to life as she sprang up, clutching at her chest and gasping for air. Josh's doctor instincts kicked in, and he jumped to work and tried to help calm his patient.

The nurses, Natalie and Wendy, came rushing in.

"It's okay, relax. We're just here to help." Josh gripped Mrs. Kors's hand.

She recognized his face and nodded, allowing him to lower her back down.

"What happened?" Natalie fumbled with her stethoscope and began to take Mrs. Kors's vitals.

"She woke up!"

Wendy gave him a look.

Mrs. Kors had been in an induced coma to keep her weak heart from overexerting itself. Josh wondered if his spell had eradicated the infection or simply taken away the strain it put on her heart. He had lost the magical precision he'd once had.

Natalie wrapped her stethoscope around her neck. "Heart

rate is normal."

"Look at this!" Wendy had pulled down the neck of Mrs. Kors's hospital gown to where the incision scar had been not even ten minutes ago. There was no sign of any lacerations at all. "She just had surgery last week!"

"What is it? What's going on?" Mrs. Kors strained to see what the other three were looking at.

Natalie tugged her gown back into place and took her hand. "How are you feeling?"

"Confused."

Josh smiled. She had always been blunt.

"You're very lucky, Mrs. Kors," he said. "Natalie and Wendy are going to run a few more tests, so just sit tight. I've got some rounds to make, but I'll be back to see you later."

The old woman smiled, still unsure of what had happened, and Josh left.

* * *

Since Chris and Holly's divorce after that mysterious fire two years ago, Josh's family had crumpled. Even before that, they weren't as close as they had been when they were younger. Since he started medical school, Josh had less and less free time. Now that his Aunt Kathy was basically the only one left, he wondered if achieving the steps to help people on a daily basis was even worth it. Especially since he had been helping people with his magic from the day his mother had died. It was a part of him that had taken a back seat since he'd started med school.

The debate over what his family life would be like if he hadn't become a doctor was irrelevant, really. Chris and Holly's divorce had caused a rift that sent shock waves through the whole family. Sophia, his little niece, had died unexpectedly, which obviously created tension for Chris and Holly. But there was something more to their separation. Josh just didn't know what. From what he could tell, Chris and Holly never spoke again after Sophia died. That wasn't just a normal breakup.

Soon after, Chris had disappeared. Didn't say a word to anyone. By the time Kathy had gotten in touch with him—when Chris finally answered his phone—it had been a week later and he had hitchhiked to Chicago. Said it was just a brief break from the real world.

That had been two years ago.

At first, Chris had kept Josh and Kathy updated on where he was: Chicago, Milwaukee, Minneapolis, Denver. He seemed to be traveling west for whatever reason.

Eventually, he stopped taking their calls. It had been over a year since Josh had talked to him. He missed him.

More importantly, he was worried about him. The last time they'd talked, Chris had mentioned that it wasn't safe to maintain connections with Erie. He'd offered no other details, and with Josh's work and Kathy's budding publishing career, they'd become too busy to look into vague leads.

That, of course, made Josh feel guilty, which may have been part of the reason he'd pulled away from his magical side. If he couldn't even be bothered to help his brother, why did he even deserve his powers? He tried to convince himself that by being a doctor he was helping more people, but the ones who mattered to him he let slip from his life. He felt ashamed.

For all Josh knew, Chris was dead. Kathy had stopped having visions of him—or at least stopped telling Josh about them—and Holly didn't want to have anything to do with the Harpers anymore. Apparently, just being in Erie was too much of a reminder of everything she had lost.

Luckily for everyone, the Harpers were still feared by most of the evil world for killing several demonic leaders ten years ago. They were unaware that the Harpers were now scattered. Distracted. Unfocused. If anyone was brave enough to attack, they would be sitting ducks. Especially Josh.

* * *

"Miss Heath, how are you today?" Josh asked his next patient.

"Bored." Another blunt one. She was a black woman who had her hair in braids. They were covered by a white bandana that matched her white blouse. Miss Heath's mother sat in the corner.

He smiled. "Your mother says you've been having fainting spells, and according to the tests we ran," he flipped a page in her chart, "you have an irregular heartbeat. A severe one at that."

"I told her, and I'll tell you, I'm fine!" She waved her hands around as she spoke, pointing to her mother and to Josh. "Listen,

I don't mean to be rude, but I'm just not a fan of Western medicine. I don't want to pump my body full of chemicals."

Josh nodded. "I understand. I know you've been taking herbal remedies—"

"Mm-hmm! I have this friend who has always been able to make me natural stuff that actually works. I've never even had an aspirin!"

On her chart, she had listed soothsayer as her occupation. This was a woman who was familiar with the magic of natural remedies—but they only went so far, in Josh's experience. Not to mention, if she wasn't truly magical, whatever concoctions her friend was whipping up wouldn't necessarily have the best effect.

"Marianne, just listen to him," her mother chirped from the corner.

"Mama, please!"

Josh bit his upper lip and played with his hospital lanyard. "Um, perhaps you should give us a minute?" He hoped that without Marianne's mother acknowledging everything he said, it wouldn't look like she was being ganged up on. This woman's heart condition was serious, but the proper care could more effectively treat it.

When her mother stepped out of the room and Josh had closed the door, he asked, "How are you really feeling?"

"I told you, I'm fine."

Josh nodded, trying to hide his growing frustration. "Okay, why don't we try a little test? I want you to compare my pulse to yours. Then you make the decision if you need further treatment from us."

The woman rolled her eyes. "Okay."

Pulling up his sleeve, Josh held out his wrist for Marianne and helped her find his pulse. As she counted, her face became serious, and she squeezed his wrist harder.

"Ooh, that's a little tight, Miss Heath. You can't really get an accurate—"

"Dr. Harper, you're in danger! I—I don't know what it is, exactly, but something is coming that will threaten you." She closed her eyes and shook her head. "It's something bigger than us. Supernatural, maybe. Certainly divine."

Josh's mouth hung open. He didn't know what to say. She wasn't possessed. Her words were her own. He could tell by her eyes.

She held her grip on his wrist until Josh's pager buzzed.

His pulled his arm back. "I've gotta go. I'm sorry, Miss Heath. I'll send one of the nurses in to check on you."

* * *

"How'd it go with your weirdo patient?" Natalie asked as they sat down to lunch.

Even though she had only started a week ago, she had weaseled her way into Josh's life. Ordinarily, he ate lunch alone. But on her first day, Natalie had plopped herself down next to him and kicked up a conversation, despite Josh's obvious social cues that he would rather eat in peace. After some awkward one-sided conversations, he now enjoyed her company.

"What weirdo patient?"

She pointed her plastic spoon at him before digging it into her yogurt cup. "You know which one. She was cleansing Wendy's aura earlier." She smiled. "I swear, Wendy was about to cut a bitch."

Josh laughed. He could imagine how that had gone down. Wendy was only interested in doing her job, not making any friends. "Oh, yeah. She was okay."

"She didn't read your fortune or anything? I could tell from the five minutes I spoke with her that she does *not* want to be here."

Josh shrugged and unscrewed the cap from his water bottle. "She took the prescription I wrote for her."

"That's good. Let's see if she takes it."

Josh mumbled, "Mm-hmm."

"You know, that stuff has always been interesting to me. Like, I know how medicine and science work and all that, but what is the thinking behind these people who rely on holistic solutions? If I'm in pain, pump me with drugs!" She laughed.

"Well, I sort of come from that world, so I get it. Still, those remedies can only go so far."

"Wait a minute! *You* come from tree-hugging la-la land?"

Josh rolled his eyes. "Not exactly, but my family has always been very…spiritual, I guess."

"Like the-big-guy-upstairs spiritual? I don't peg you as that type of guy."

Josh raised an eyebrow. "There's a lot about me you don't know." She narrowed her eyes at him and he continued, "No, my family has always been intuitive, I suppose."

"Like…divination?"

In response, he shrugged. This conversation was getting too close to home for his taste, but Natalie had a way of dragging pieces of information out of him.

She put up her hands. "Hold on. You're telling me that you believe in all that psychic crap? How the hell did you make it through med school?"

Josh rolled his eyes again. "I said my family relies on it. I'm different. Divination hasn't been kind to me. Especially when there are facts to prove an answer."

"Yeah, yeah. You like black-and-white answers. Medicine isn't exactly black and white, though."

"It is more so than divination."

"Okay, so can you read my palm or look into a crystal ball or something and tell me when I'm going to get married? How many kids I'm going to have?"

"Crystal ball? Really?"

She shrugged. "Hey, I don't know how you psychics do it."

"Yeah, no, I can't. Divination is more fluid. You can't necessarily control it. Sometimes it just hits you—from what I've experienced, at least. Like today, Miss Heath must've seen something during my exam. It was weird." He saw a smile creep across Natalie's face and regretted his last statement.

"I see you've left the juicy parts out of my original question."

She waved her fingers toward her. "Explain."

"Well, she was convinced that she was fine, so I wanted to compare my heart rate to hers—"

"You had her feel you up?"

He pointed to his wrist. "My pulse, dodo."

"Right."

"But something weird happened when she took my wrist."

"Do I wanna hear this?"

"Just shut up and let me finish. She got real serious—I've seen that look before—and she told me I was in danger."

"And...?"

He shrugged. "And that's it. I got freaked out and left. She didn't say anything when I gave her the prescription, but her mother was there, so maybe she didn't want to talk about it then."

"Or maybe she's just nuts? Listen, I'm not trying to knock your family's beliefs or anything, but how in the world could that woman—who's never met you before—know that you're in danger? It doesn't make sense."

"But what if she's right?"

"She's probably not." She reached across the table and took his hand. "Look, if I had a dollar for every fortune I was told that came true, I don't think I'd be changing bedpans for a living." Natalie was from New York City and came to Erie for Gannon's nursing program. She had plenty of stories about her encounters with crazy. "I think your stress level is making you overthink this. The woman is bonkers, and you need to relax."

Josh leaned back in his chair and stretched. "Yeah, I know.

But easier said than done. I'm working doubles today and to-morrow, and then this weekend I need to read over the journals I've been putting off."

"Okay, this is what you're going to do: work your doubles, sleep in this weekend—no exceptions—and then Saturday night you can pick me up from here and we're going out for a late dinner. You can read your journals all day, but you need a night off from everything to really relax."

He began to shake his head. "I don't think—"

"That's it! Don't think! Just make sure you're here right at nine when I get out. I really hate waiting." She stood and picked up her tray. "I've gotta get back to work. Make sure you think of someplace nice to take me. I've got standards, you know."

* * *

"Hey, honey, I just wanted to call and tell you I'm on my way home now," Kathy said.

It was Josh's day off, and he had done what Natalie had told him. He'd slept in and spent the day catching up on his reading. He had taken a break to look for a decent place to take Natalie—she hadn't said whether it was a date or not, so he didn't want to assume anything.

Josh was figuring out what to wear when his aunt called. It had been a long time since he had been out for something that wasn't related to work. Usually when he was home he wore sweatpants and an old T-shirt because he was either sleeping or studying. If he went out, it was usually to a gala or fundraiser that required his attendance as part of the Cardiology Department. He didn't have any appropriate casual attire.

"How was your trip?"

Kathy had been in New York City for the week meeting with her publisher and planning the promotional launch of her latest book. With as much as Josh was working, he'd barely even noticed.

"Good. Very good. There's something I need to discuss with you, though, when I get home—a couple of things, actually."

"Okay." He contemplated two shirts. "Hey, what is the dress code for dinner with a coworker?"

"A date? Josh, your last date was when you were an undergrad. What was that? Like, six or seven years ago?"

"It's not a date." He rubbed his forehead, regretting mentioning anything. "At least, I don't think so. It wasn't explicitly said."

"Well who asked who?"

"She asked me."

"Who is it?"

"A nurse."

"That's all you're going to give me? I've got a long ride back, and I don't think I have a big enough book to cover it!"

"I think a tie is too formal, don't you think?" Josh ignored her teasing.

"That depends, is she a formal girl?"

"I don't know. All I've seen her in are scrubs." He looked at his choice of ties. "On second thought, I don't like these ties. Do you think a T-shirt is too casual?"

"What about a sweater?"

"That's true." He pushed aside clothes in his closet. "I should've done laundry today."

Kathy laughed. "You're nervous, aren't you?"

"Well, you said it: I haven't been on a date since I was twenty years old. She probably already thinks I'm a freak. I don't want to encourage that."

"Why does she think you're a freak?"

Josh considered telling Kathy about Miss Heath's warning but decided against it. There was nothing she could do about it on the train. She would probably suggest he stay home and away from anything dangerous, and Josh didn't want to cancel on Natalie. He was nervous. But also excited.

"Nothing. Look, I have to go. I love you and I hope you have a safe trip back. I'm working tomorrow morning, so I probably won't see you until I get home. Text me when you do get home, though."

"Yes, sir! Have fun on your date. Remember, the house is all yours tonight."

"Okay bye!"

* * *

"Well this is certainly better than I was expecting," Natalie said.

Josh had picked a steakhouse in the Presque Isle Downs and Casino. Because of the late hour, the place was basically empty.

Only a few people still lingered.

"I gotta be honest, when you started heading out of the city, I thought you were going to chop me up and bury me in a farm field because I exposed your secret."

Josh smiled. "What secret?"

"Your family's voodoo ways." She wiggled her fingers.

"Oh. That's not really a huge secret. In fact, we've sort of stopped with all of that."

"How come? I thought it was like a religion sort of thing?"

"Not exactly. But once I went to college and my brother got divorced and moved away—and my aunt's book deal—we all kind of have our own thing going on."

"So you guys used to be really close?"

Josh nodded. "Chris and I have always been close—up until the last few years or so. But ever since my mom died, it's kind of been my aunt, my brother, and I against the world. That's not the case anymore."

"Aw, I'm sorry."

Anxious to get away from his sob story, Josh asked, "What about you? It's gotta be tough being so far away from your family."

"When you're raised in a city like New York, family is more of a general term. My mom was a single parent and worked three jobs to pay the rent, so I kind of grew up with the neighborhood kids. But we lived in the projects. Families were in and out of there all the time. I've been friends with people in Erie a lot longer than I've been friends with some people from New York."

"Oh, wow. I thought my story was sad!"

She rolled her eyes. "Yeah, yeah. Poor Natalie. So where did your brother move to?"

"Out west. Last I talked to him he was in Utah."

"He moves around a lot?"

"Oh yeah."

"Wow, what does he do? I mean, his job must be pretty flexible then. Online stuff? Truck driver?"

"Um…" Josh didn't want to lie any more than he had to, but the truth sounded too suspicious: Why wouldn't Josh know what his brother did for a living if all he'd done was move away? "He worked at a steel plant when he lived here, so I would assume he's doing something like that there. We don't really talk about his job. I actually haven't talked to him in a while."

"How come?"

"Busy."

She smiled. "But you made time for me."

"I think I remember *you* clearing my evening."

She waved her hand at him. "Details."

The rest of dinner went smoothly. Josh relaxed as the evening progressed. Natalie was beautiful, funny, smart—Josh seemed to like her more and more with each new piece of information he learned about her. She was easy to talk to.

When they left the restaurant, Natalie asked, "So what's next on the agenda?"

Josh stammered. He didn't realize he needed to plan a whole evening of festivities.

He cleared his throat. "Well, uh, we could walk the casino a bit? Maybe play some games?"

Natalie scrunched her nose. "I'm not one for gambling."

"We could go back to my place—to watch a movie or something. I'm not assuming anything here." Josh's face flushed.

"Hmm, that's too bad. Yeah, we could go to your place."

"Really?"

"Yeah. I've never been to a voodoo house before."

"It's not—"

"I get it, Josh. Let's go."

Outside, the air was cold. They both buried their hands in their pockets and walked quickly to Josh's car.

Halfway across the parking lot, the ground began to shake. Natalie grasped Josh's arm for support, and they both struggled to stay on their feet.

"What's going on? Is it an earthquake?"

"In Pennsylvania?" Josh muttered. A light post fell onto a line of cars, setting off an alarm and eliminating the light in their immediate area.

"You've been pretty quiet lately," a woman's voice said. Josh looked around but couldn't place where it was coming from. "Hiding in plain sight. But your little use of magic the other day was just what I needed to find you." She stepped into view, but her face was still shrouded by shadows.

"Who are you?" Josh asked. He wanted to get Natalie out of there to protect her. And his secret.

"My name's Collie. I'm part of an elite alliance we thought

you might want to join, but it seems you're not as strong as you once were." She chuckled. "Pretty pathetic that you peaked as a teenager."

"Listen, we're not hurting anybody. Just let us go home," Josh pleaded.

"No. I want a duel. Goldilocks can watch."

"Why?"

"I need to test the strength of your powers."

He kept his eyes on Collie. He didn't want to duel for a number of reasons, but a major one was that he didn't know what kind of power he had anymore. He'd stopped using his magic actively since he'd first started college nine years ago.

"Josh, what is she talking about?" Natalie asked.

"I'm not joining any club."

Collie stomped her foot, sending a crack in the pavement all the way to Josh and Natalie. They both collapsed on the ground from the tremors. "Yes, you are!"

Josh pulled his keys out of his pocket and handed them to Natalie. "Get to the car and be careful. I'll be there soon."

"What? No!"

"Just go! I'll be fine." He didn't believe the words himself, but he thought he made it sound convincing.

Once Natalie had raced off between the cars, Josh stood and faced Collie.

"You trying to expose me?"

"I'm just trying to test your powers." She waved her hands toward her. "Come at me with your best shot."

Sucking on his bottom lip, Josh dug deep to the subdued power source within him. He channeled it into the palms of his hands. What had once been so easy. With a surge of power, he created a blast that pushed Collie back a few steps.

Her reaction terrified Josh. He had summoned all the strength he could muster.

"Oh." Collie sounded surprised. "That was it, huh?" She bent her knees and lifted her arms up, making the ground shake and knocking Josh off balance again. He toppled to the pavement.

Struggling to stand, Josh tried to focus on the magic within him again and create a bigger gust of wind. He waved his arms, and Collie was thrown back into the car behind her. That was certainly better than the first attempt.

"Maybe you just need to be motivated!" Collie slid off the car and stomped on the ground again. Another crack formed in the pavement and traveled toward Josh. His foot was almost caught in it, but he stepped aside in time.

Throwing his hands in her direction, Josh created a small tornado that sent Collie rolling over the car behind her. When she came around again, her face was bloody and her breaths were heavy.

"Well, I think I have everything I need."

"What does that mean?" Josh asked, but she ran off.

Back at his car, Natalie wrapped him in a hug when she saw that he was okay. She squeezed him hard. "If you were gone any longer, I was gonna call the cops. Should we?"

Josh shook his head. "No, I'm fine. She's the one that's bleeding. I don't need a criminal charge against me."

She nodded. "Okay. Let's get out of here. I'm so freaked out."

* * *

Except for the pop music playing softly on the radio, the car ride was silent. When they got to Josh's house, he made her a cup of tea to help calm her nerves and they sat on the couch.

"So that was weird," Josh started. He didn't want to ask her what she'd heard in case she hadn't heard anything, but he also wanted to clear the air and put to bed any suspicions she might have.

Natalie nodded and wrapped her fingers around her mug. "She seemed to know you."

Josh shook his head. "I didn't know her. At least, I don't think I did. I meet a lot of people at work."

She still seemed nervous. Josh ran his thumb along her cheek. "Hey, we're both okay, so that's all that matters, right?"

"I can't believe I'm going to ask this, but are you…I mean, you're not…"

"What?"

She shook her head. "Never mind."

"No, what?"

She hesitated a moment longer. "You're not, like…magical or anything, right?"

Josh's heart nearly stopped. "Um…why do you ask that?"

She smiled and looked down into her mug. "Right, okay. So

that's a confirmation." She set her mug down on the coffee table and stood. "I think you're crazy. I should've known the other day when you started talking about divination and holistic remedies and everything." She muttered to herself, "Wow, okay. Looks like there's crazy everywhere." She started to the door.

"Natalie, stop!" Josh followed her. She already had the door open, so he held out his hand and created a gust of wind to slam it shut before she could step outside. Now that he had awoken his magic, it came easier to him.

She turned, wild-eyed. "What's going on?"

"You're right." He stepped closer. "I'm a witch. That's what that girl wanted today."

"How—this isn't possible."

"Come sit down. We should talk about this. It's not so crazy, really." He had never told his secret before. It felt surreal to admit it. Like he was floating in air watching himself.

Once they were back on the couch, he searched for the right way to start the conversation. He had hidden his magic his entire life. So well that he almost felt guilty for acknowledging it.

"Well, magic is real."

"Yeah, I got that. So you really are a freak."

"No. Look, I've had magic my whole life. When I was younger, my family and I would use it to help people by going after the things that the nonmagical couldn't."

"So why did you stop?"

Josh shrugged. "The biggest threats were gone. My aunt still chases down the bad guys from time to time, and my brother might too, but I'm helping people in a different way now. I haven't used magic for a while."

"Do you use magic on your patients?"

Josh shook his head. "No."

Natalie cocked an eyebrow. "Then when did you last use magic?"

He shrugged.

Natalie crossed her arms. "That woman said you used it the other day. That's how she was able to find you."

So she had heard something.

"Oh. Yeah, I did a little spell on Mrs. Kors."

"The woman in her eighties who had pacemaker complications? You saved her? That's how she woke up, isn't it?"

Josh closed his eyes and sighed. He very rarely used magic at work. Only on the extreme cases: a family car accident, a little girl's cancer, a man about to miss the birth of his first grandchild. He didn't want Natalie to assume he did it all the time.

"So why wouldn't you use it on Mr. Douglas last month? He didn't deserve to live but your neighbor did?"

Mr. Douglas had had a heart attack when he was home alone. It was about an hour before anyone found him. The paramedics had revived him on the way to the hospital, but by the time Josh and the rest of the team got to him, his heart was failing. He died soon after.

"That's not what it is. What I did with Mrs. Kors was wrong. I shouldn't have done that. It's not my place to play God. I just couldn't watch her die."

"Then assign her to another doctor."

"I should have, I'm sorry."

They were quiet, but Josh could tell Natalie was still upset with him.

After a few minutes, he asked, "So that's all you're going to question me on? How I use magic at work?"

She shrugged. "You said you and your family help people. You're helping people the normal way now. I believe you. Your using magic on patients is wrong, but you've admitted that. I do have another question, though."

"What's that?"

"If you're able to help people magically, why do you do it medically? I would think the supernatural way is the faster way."

"Well, magic has limitations. You can't heal everything. You can't bring someone back from the dead. There are also a lot of bad people using magic—like Collie today. Magic can be dangerous. My mom died because of magic. So did my niece. It's not all Harry Potter mysticism."

"Oh. I didn't know they died because of magic. I can see why you gave it up. But—and I don't know this for sure—but isn't magic a part of you? Like, if I decided to stop being a nurse. If I saw someone hurt, my nurse brain is going to kick in and I'm going to go to work. How can you keep your magic so subdued?"

Josh shrugged. "Practice. Like I said, I haven't used it in so long, and the limitations and repercussions remind me that it's not to be taken lightly."

"So magic kind of sucks."

He laughed. "It can, yeah."

Another silence fell upon them. Natalie played with the fringe on the throw draped over the back of the couch. Josh's hands fidgeted as he wondered what else he could say.

Natalie was the first to break the silence. "Uh, when I was… oh, about nine or so, my neighbor and I were playing outside, as usual. It was Easter Sunday. We had just found our baskets filled with candy, and we immediately went outside to show everyone and trade—all the cool kids had solid-filled bunny rabbits. The lame ones were hollow."

"Of course!"

"Anyway, so everyone slowly got called in for dinner. Eventually, it was just me and another girl left. Our moms were working, so we didn't have a dinner curfew. She had just traded three rolls of Smarties for six purple Jolly Ranchers—"

"The worst flavor, ever! Tastes like cough syrup."

She flashed a sad smile and continued, "I didn't realize she had popped one in her mouth. We were running around outside and she just stopped. I asked her what was wrong, but she didn't say anything—couldn't." Natalie bit her bottom lip and looked up at Josh. "I was frozen. I didn't know what to do. I didn't want to leave her alone, but I didn't know the Heimlich then. Eventually, another neighbor spotted us and ran over. He saved that girl's life."

"Wow. I'm sorry."

"I felt so helpless. I didn't want to ever feel helpless again. That's why I became a nurse. To help people." She wiped at her eyes. "I suppose you've never felt that way before. You can do anything."

He shook his head. "I watched my mother die when I was sixteen." He pointed. "Right over there. It was a demon who did it. I had active powers then, but I just wasn't strong enough. I tried, but it didn't matter. So yeah, I have felt helpless. It's a part of life sometimes, I suppose."

Natalie took Josh's hand and leaned in and kissed him.

"Sorry for calling you a freak."

"You reacted just as I predicted—better, actually." He squeezed her hand. "You're still here."

She smiled and laid her head on his shoulder. "Despite everything I learned about you tonight—lots of stuff—I still like you. You are a very interesting individual, Josh Harper."

He chuckled. "Well, thanks. I'm glad you found out. At least I can talk to someone about it. Besides the people at the hospital, I only really see my aunt, and that's in passing."

Natalie sat up and placed her hand over her heart. "I make a vow to be someone you see more than just in passing. I'm going to be your shadow. Wherever you go, I go."

"That could get creepy."

"I'm a weird girl, Josh. But you don't have a choice. You're stuck with me."

"Is this your way of getting a second date?"

She smiled. "*I'm* not asking."

"Would you like to go on a second date sometime?"

"We haven't even finished the first one yet!"

He raised his eyebrows. "Yeah? What did you have in mind?"

She stood and took his hand. "You're a doctor. I think you're smart enough to figure it out."

* * *

"How was your trip?" Josh asked the next evening when he got home. Kathy was washing the dishes when he walked in.

"Not as eventful as your night last night," Kathy said.

He gave her a quick sideways hug. "What do you mean?"

"I'm just assuming." She flashed a smile. "But never mind that. My third book is going to be awesome. With any luck, I'll get on the New York Times best seller list."

"That's awesome!"

"Yeah, and my editor and I discussed ideas for my fourth book as well."

"Hey, you might as well keep going," Josh said. "I'm really happy for you. That's great."

Kathy scrubbed away at a plate and kept her eyes down. "Um…there's something else I need to talk to you about."

"Yeah, I've got something to tell you too."

"Mine's more important. Holly called."

DECEPTION

A SHORT STORY

DAVID NETH

DECEPTION

The Magician.
The High Priestess.
The Emperor reversed.
The Lovers.
Strength reversed.
The Fool reversed.
The Moon.

By now, Holly was so well versed in the basic spread of the major arcana that she knew what the reading meant: she previously had skill and diplomacy, but also pain and loss. She currently held secrets, and her future would be filled with benevolence and compassion, but also obstruction and unknown enemies. The advice was love and attraction—something Holly's life had been empty of for two years. The influences to her future were an abuse of power and weakness, and her hopes and fears were apathy and carelessness. Finally, her overall outcome would be danger, darkness, deception, and terror.

She picked up the cards and reshuffled. Something had to be off. She must not be focusing on the right thing. The second drawing resulted in the same cards in the same exact order.

Redrawing again a third time had the same results. This reading was true. There was no denying that anymore. Now she needed to figure out what it meant.

When she'd first come to Lily Dale after her divorce, she had kept to herself for the most part. Establishing new connections with the people in the town she now called home would only lead to heartbreak—that had been evident her whole life. Everyone she loved eventually left her or betrayed her: Drew, her father, Sophia, and Chris.

Drew hadn't intentionally left her. He was killed. There was nothing she could do to stop it, no matter how many "What if?" scenarios she ran through. Prior to that, he had been trying to distance himself from Holly for her protection. She could see that now. Ever since the Fire Wizards' corruption, he had viewed himself as poison to her. There had been nothing she could do to change his mind.

She sometimes wondered what would've happened if the Fire Wizards had never turned. Would Drew still be alive? Would she have married him instead?

Holly's father was a different story. Simon had a life already established in Salem. So did Holly, until her world was flipped around when she'd learned she was a witch. Not long after, she'd been on a bus to Erie. She had never been the same. She couldn't always tell if she had changed for the better, though. Sometimes she wished she was the naïve little girl she had been all those years ago. Back when things were simpler. Easier.

Chris was the reason she had stayed in Erie. Well, him and his family, but Chris was certainly the anchor. If she had known then what he would do, she never would have pursued the relationship. Loving him brought her the most pain and heartache she had ever experienced. It further separated her from her friends in Salem—who were living completely normal lives by now. Holly wouldn't know. She hadn't been back to Salem since her father had passed away five years ago. Lori and the rest of her friends were strangers to her now.

The thing about her father's death was that it had been completely natural. He was never the same after his stroke. After two years as a vegetable, he had finally been reunited with his wife. That was the silver lining to Simon's death.

The deaths of everyone else in Holly's family had been the results of something supernatural. Even people she had known who weren't her family—Margaret, Drew—their deaths had been at the hands of Will. She never would've lost Margaret and Drew if she hadn't been so damn infatuated with Chris. She hated herself for being so lovesick.

Her Uncle Ken, the only other survivor of the Bowen family, hadn't stuck around Salem. After he had been returned to his human form when Toxanna had been killed, he continued his nomadic ways and set off traveling the world once more. Apparently, before Holly's mother had died, he had studied witch cultures in Europe and Africa. The last postcard he'd sent was from Australia. That was six months ago. She wondered what kind of information he was learning and if he intended to share it with her. She was once again the youngest member of the Bowen line. If she ever had more children, she would pass that knowledge on.

Additional children were unlikely, but in Holly's experience, she had learned to never say never. They had just passed the two-year anniversary of Sophia's death. Josh and Kathy had both tried to call. Holly knew they'd want to reminisce and remind her that they still considered her family despite any issues she might have with Chris. It was sweet, but she couldn't stand to continue to be associated with Chris on any level. He had committed the ultimate betrayal—killing their daughter.

At the time, Chris's specialty had expanded and allowed him to wield flame. He'd been obsessed with getting stronger. Sure, he worked to make a living, but magic was his passion. After Sophia was born, Holly stopped looking for enemies. Once she became a mother, she had wanted to eliminate that danger so her daughter wouldn't grow up without a mother.

Not like she had.

The night of the accident, Holly had run to the grocery store. Chris wanted the evening to spend with Sophia. He had been working overtime a lot to help pay for the house they had just bought. Holly had thought a daddy-daughter night was a great idea.

Oh, how she'd been wrong.

When she came back, fire trucks blocked the street. She

needed to park several houses down and walk home. As she approached her house, she saw that it was engulfed in flames. She tried to run inside, but a fireman stopped her. He directed her to Chris, who was receiving oxygen in the back of an ambulance.

Sophia was nowhere to be found. She could tell by the look in Chris's eyes that he had left her in there. The blue and gold flames indicated that they were magical. How could Chris be so stupid to practice his pyro abilities with their daughter in the house?

Holly had taken off running back to her car and driven off, staying at a hotel until deciding to move to Lily Dale. She hadn't spoken to Chris since that day, nor did she want to. She hated him and wanted to forget that their marriage ever happened. Most importantly, she just wanted her daughter back.

* * *

The doorbell rang. Holly's four o'clock appointment. Ordinarily, she sat on the front porch so she wouldn't have to bring people into her house, but it was too cold even for her enclosed front patio. She had laid out a tablecloth and lit a couple of candles—not completely necessary, but they added to the aesthetic people wanted whenever they came to Lily Dale.

"Helen?" Holly asked when she answered the door.

"That's me." She was an older woman with her gray hair tucked under a plastic hood to protect her perm.

"Why don't you come in and we can get started?"

Once they were seated, Holly listened as Helen took the liberty of divulging her complete family history. She also threw in her previous experience with spiritualism and how many readings she had received, which was typical for most of Holly's clients.

Altogether, the recap took a half an hour—much longer than Holly cared to chat, but she kept a smile on her face the whole time. It was a rough day for her. Memories of Sophia popped up everywhere, and she was having a hard time concentrating.

"So what are you searching for today?"

"My sister, Jeanie, has been sick for a long time," Helen started.

Holly nodded. "Yeah, you told me. I'm sorry to hear that."

"I'm her health proxy, and it looks like we are going to have to make some difficult decisions soon."

Now Helen had Holly's full attention. Everyone who Holly had lost had been at someone else's hands or something else out of her control. She had never lost anyone by her own choice. The fact that Helen had to choose whether or not her sister lived or died was something Holly couldn't relate to. Her heart went out to the woman.

"Oh."

Helen nodded again. "So that's what I'm hoping to figure out today to help me make my decision."

Holly kept her eyes on her client for a moment. She didn't want Helen to put all of her faith in Holly's reading, especially since she wasn't fully focused today. She couldn't have that on her conscience, and she didn't want Helen to make a poor choice simply because Holly was having an off day. Even if she was on her A-game, readings weren't definite at all.

THE CRESCENT MOON

"I would tread carefu—"

Helen held up her hand. "I know what you're going to say: these things are very iffy, but I need some sort of guidance. My daughter's telling me one thing, the doctor is telling me another…I just don't know what to do. I need some sort of clarity."

Holly gripped Helen's hand and nodded. "Of course." She passed the tarot deck off to Helen and instructed her to shuffle them. The woman didn't have the steadiest hands and Holly hated watching her struggle, but in order for the reading to be successful, Helen needed to be the one to shuffle the deck.

As her client fumbled with the cards, Holly waved her hand over the lit candle and muttered:

Guiding spirits, hear my plea,
let the answer come to me.

When Helen passed back the deck, Holly began laying the cards out, explaining what each one stood for. She liked to place all the cards on the table and walk her clients through what they stood for and how they were all related.

"The first card is your past, the second is your present, and the third—"

Helen grasped Holly's arm tightly. When she met her eyes, she saw they were glowing white. The woman was saying something quietly, but Holly couldn't make it out.

"What is it? Helen, are you all right?"

"…Chaos…"

"Chaos? Helen, what are you talking about?" She hoped that

by using her name she would draw her out of her trance faster. It didn't seem to be working, though.

"An old enemy…he's coming…never died…Chaos…"

"Helen!" Holly tried to pull the old woman's hand off her wrist, but her grip was strong. "Helen, what are you talking about? What old enemy?"

Holly worried about Toxanna and wondered if she was somehow still alive. But it had been ten years since she'd died; Holly would've found out if her family's former adversary had survived. Especially since she and her Uncle Ken were the only ones left. They would be the only targets.

What was worse was that none of what Helen was saying was related to the woman at all. How did a prophecy or whatever Helen was spewing come through with her reading and not the one Holly had been doing just before Helen had arrived?

"The Chaos is here!" Helen shouted it now and squeezed Holly's wrist even harder and began to shake.

With a quick huff, Holly blew out the candle in case it fell. The white glow in Helen's eyes dissipated, and her hold softened.

"Helen, are you all right?"

The woman looked very confused and her hands shook. "What happened?"

"You had a very powerful reading." She studied the old woman. She looked exhausted. "Is there someone who can drive you home?"

After a moment, she nodded. "My daughter is outside."

"Good. Go home and relax. That would take a lot out of anybody."

The Crescent Moon

She stood and helped Helen to the door, waving for her daughter to come and help. She watched as Helen's daughter drove away. The car was long gone before the cold began to bother Holly, and she turned to go inside.

"Are you closed for the day?"

Holly turned and saw a man coming down the walk. He was fairly attractive, if Holly was looking for that sort of thing. He appeared to be in his midtwenties—about the same age as Holly was herself. She was sure she knew him from somewhere, but she couldn't place where. Either he was a regular visitor to the community, or he just had one of those faces.

"Um…no, I guess I can take you real quick." She crossed her arms and shivered as a gust of wind came. "I'm Holly. Who are you?"

"Elliott." He placed a hand on her back and said, "Let's get inside. I don't want you getting sick."

Without realizing it, she shrugged away from his touch as they climbed the stairs into her house.

"I haven't had a chance to clean up from the last client, so I'm sorry for the mess." Holly collected the items scattered across the table.

"Don't worry about it." Elliott unwound his scarf so that it hung around his neck, but didn't take his coat off. "I've seen messier mediums. You have a very nice house."

"Well, thank you." Anxious to get him out quickly so that she could figure out Helen's words, she said, "I'm afraid I won't be able to do my traditional tarot card reading for you since the energies in the room are still so concentrated on my previous client. I could do a tea leaf reading, if you're interested."

He nodded. "That's fine. I'm more or less just feeding my curiosity."

A lot of people came through her door who were simply curious. Sometimes their readings turned into quiz time, which Holly tried to keep to a minimum. Everyone was either interested in mediumship or trying to discredit it. Oftentimes, Holly didn't have a lot of luck sticking to the reading when naysayers came around. She could tell the type, but they were still paying customers.

"Okay. Why don't you have a seat? I'll be there in a second."

She went into the kitchen and turned the stove on to heat the tea kettle.

"Where are you from?" Holly hated the awkward silence that filled the room more than she hated small talk.

"I've been lots of places. Upstate near Albany, down in Pennsylvania. I've actually just come back from the, uh, South."

"I bet it's nice down there. I've never been." She pulled down her mason jar of loose tea leaves from a shelf next to the sink and unscrewed the top. "What brings you to Lily—"

She was pressed up against the refrigerator as something sharp poked through her sweater, threatening to pierce her skin.

"You're what I'm looking for."

"Let me go!" She knew he looked familiar, but she still couldn't place from where.

"What did you learn at the last reading?"

Whipping her head back, she crashed the back of her skull into his nose and swiftly turned around and delivered a punch to his gut. She raced to the door, but hesitated. If everyone found out about the danger she brought to the community, they would kick her out. She had nowhere else to go.

She was pulled back to reality when the knife that had pressed to her back moments before struck the door, inches from her face. She turned around and saw Elliott stepping toward her. His pale skin seemed to be peeling off his face, dripping onto his jacket and rolling to the floor. He lifted his hand and tugged a piece away, revealing vibrant blue skin underneath.

"Zamball."

He smiled. It was a sickening sight as the rest of his flesh began to loosen and curl. "I bet you didn't expect this."

"How did you—I thought you were dead."

He peeled off more and more of his skin. "Tell me what you heard at the last reading, and I promise to leave you alone."

Holly narrowed her eyes. He was bluffing. He wouldn't have tracked her down solely to learn what she had discovered at her last reading. He must've been watching her for a while now, and the thought terrified her. She had grown too comfortable here in the last two years.

She raised her hand and tried to pull the knife from the door, but it wouldn't budge.

"Tell me!"

"No!"

He produced his wand and shot off a burst of water, consuming Holly in a pocket of water. She struggled to break free, but the more she moved, the more her chest burned for air.

Finally, Zamball lowered his wand, and the water pocket

burst. Holly fell to the floor and gasped for breath. She watched as he stepped closer, but her body was too weak to move. It had been a long time since she had faced this kind of magic. She was out of practice.

Zamball crouched down and seized a fistful of Holly's wet hair.

"One last chance. What do you know?"

Holly propped herself up so his grip didn't hurt as bad and met his eyes. "Why would I tell you? You can't kill me. Then you'll never know what happened."

"You underestimate just what I'm looking for. Besides, I know you have a family."

"*Had* a family."

He smiled. "You and I both know just how much you and the Harpers still care for one another. I know your husband is off the grid, but his brother and aunt are still fair game."

"They have nothing to do with this!"

"Wrong!" His grip tightened. "They helped start this! Now if they're not motivation enough for you, I know you have an uncle who is currently in Sydney. I could pay him a visit. I don't think I've ever formally met him. His guard would be down and—"

"Okay! Okay, I'll tell you. Just let me go, first." Her chest was still heaving, but for the moment she was focused on the hold he had on her hair.

He tugged a little harder. "*Don't* mess with me."

"I won't!"

A moment later he released her, and she pulled away from him.

The Crescent Moon

"The reading?"

Waving her hand, the room began to rapidly fill with water.

"Is this supposed to stop me? Do you realize what my specialty is?"

Holly backed away from him and watched as the water reached their knees and climbed higher.

Zamball pulled out his wand. "You're just giving me ammunition to drown you. After all these years, you're still just a stupid little girl. Too bad the Harpers aren't here to save you this time."

He waved his wand and pointed it at Holly, but still, the water continued to rise. He looked around, flabbergasted. Trying again to no avail, he attempted to fuel his magic with a spell:

Just as quickly as the water will rise,
I command it to go where I decide!

His words had no effect, and the water continued to fill the room.

"You see, I have a specialty too, Zamball." Holly smirked. "It took me a while to figure out what it was and even longer to appreciate it, but it definitely comes in handy."

"Is this water hexed?"

"You could say that. Either way, your magic can't control it. I'm the only one who can. I want you to leave and never come back. Otherwise, I'm going to let you die."

"You're a foolish witch. You're just as trapped as I am."

Holly shook her head and crossed her arms as the water reached her chest. "I'm really not. You have about five minutes before it will be above your head."

Zamball narrowed his eyes. "This is far from over!" He waded over to a window and jammed his elbow into it a few times until it gave. He turned and offered Holly a smile before kicking out the window further and jumping through.

As the water reached her head, she waved her hand and it disappeared without a sign that it had ever filled her house. Peeking her head outside, she saw a few of her neighbors looking in her direction. This would be difficult to clean up.

* * *

"Holly?" Kathy sounded confused. It had been a long time since Holly had spoken with her. Longer since Holly had been the one to reach out.

"Yeah. Something happened—a couple of things, actually."

"Are you okay?"

Holly nodded. "Yeah. Just a little shaken up, I guess."

After she'd called one of her neighbors to board up her window, she had taken a shower until the hot water ran out. She had a chill that she couldn't get rid of. Whether that had been from her wet clothes or fear, she wasn't sure.

Her world was once again flipped on her in a single day. She'd thought she was safe in Lily Dale and had been attempting to piece her life back together, but now it was apparent that that was impossible.

"Tell me what happened."

Holly didn't even know where to start. The day had been so

long and so much had happened. She decided to start with Helen's reading and the warning.

"Wow," Kathy said after Holly was done.

"I know."

"No, I just got the same warning. Might've even seen it, actually."

"What?"

"Yeah, I'm on my way back from New York City, and some guy was screaming about the Chaos at the train station. I blew him off at first, but he looked directly at me and said my name."

"What do you think it is?" Holly couldn't understand why she and Kathy would receive the same message. She wondered if any other witches had been warned. Did Josh know too? Did Chris?

"I don't know. Not good, that's for sure. I'm still on my way back. Once I get home I'm going to talk to Josh and look in the book."

"Yeah, that's a good idea."

"You should come back—"

"No," Holly interrupted. "I can't."

Kathy sighed. "Holly, if you got the message, then you're in danger too. I know things ended badly with you and Chris. You both lost a lot. It hurt him too. He hasn't been home in two years. We haven't even spoken to him in the last year."

"Oh."

Holly was genuinely surprised. She knew Chris felt defeated. Whether Sophia's death had been intentional or not didn't matter. He had killed her, and Holly knew he wouldn't be able to live with himself.

She just didn't realize he would completely abandon his family. She almost hated him more because of it. Why would he punish his family for the mistakes he'd made?

"You're always welcome here. I really hope you come back. Josh and I miss you. You have friends here."

"Yeah." Holly wasn't sure if she could even face Josh and Kathy again. She was just damning Chris for abandoning his family, but hadn't she done the same thing? Although her marriage to Chris had been short, the Harpers had been her family. Besides her uncle, they were the closest thing she had to one.

"I know it's a big choice because you probably have your life settled elsewhere by now, but just keep it in mind. We'd take you back in a second."

"Thanks. I'll think about it."

"Good. Make sure you be careful."

"Well, there's actually more I want to tell you."

"What is it?"

Holly sighed and debated the best way to approach the subject. If Kathy knew that she had been attacked, she would make sure Holly moved back to Erie simply for protection. At the moment, the idea didn't seem so bad. Her large empty house intimidated her, and she wished she didn't live alone, even though she wanted to be left alone. Comfortable silence was what she was after, and she knew the Harpers understood that with events like these.

But moving back to Erie would mean constant demonic threats. Something she had been free of for the last two years.

However, if Zamball's attack was a sign of the future, things had changed, and she would need the extra help. She had been through enough to know she couldn't do it alone.

"Holly, are you okay?"

Feeling the lump forming in her throat, she said, "Not really."

"Why? What happened?"

"Zamball is still alive."

"Did he hurt you?"

Holly shook her head at first and then added, "Not really, no. But he seemed very interested in the warning about the Chaos. I just don't know how he found me! I've been so careful!"

"I know, sweetie, I know. Is that all he wanted?"

"Yeah. But he knows about you guys and he knows Chris hasn't been in Erie for a while. He's been watching us. How do I know if there's anyone else watching?"

She felt like an idiot for crying on the phone to a woman she hadn't spoken with in a year, but she needed someone to comfort her and she had no one else. She had lived in Lily Dale for two years, but nobody really knew anything about her. Truth be told, she was lonely. She thought she didn't need anyone, but after today she realized she was wrong. Very wrong.

"Why don't you cast a protection spell on your house? Do you have one?"

"I think, yeah." Like her mother, Holly kept lots of journals containing her magical knowledge. She had been meaning to get a nice book like the Harpers' but hadn't gotten around to it.

"Okay good. Use that and keep an eye out for any suspicious

activity. Call me or Josh if something comes up. Do you still have Josh's number?"

"Yeah."

"Okay good. Put us on speed dial."

"Okay."

"Holly."

"Yeah?"

"I know it's going to be difficult, but now I would strongly recommend you move back here. At least until we have all this nonsense with the Chaos and Zamball straightened out."

Holly smiled. She liked Kathy for a number of reasons, but one of the main reasons was that she didn't make decisions for anyone.

"I think we've all gotten a little lazy over the years, but we can't slip up now," Kathy continued. "I don't want you getting hurt just because you were alone. Remember how much we needed each other with Toxanna and Will?"

Holly nodded. "You're right. I'll talk to the board here and see what my options are. Lily Dale isn't safe for me anymore, and I don't want to bring my problems here. They're not properly equipped for it."

"You're in Lily Dale?"

Holly cringed. She had just given away her location, something she had tried to protect since moving here. But it didn't matter anymore. She had just decided she was leaving. Moving back to Erie. She would certainly need strength for that.

"I'll call you soon to let you know how I'm doing."

"Okay good."

The Crescent Moon

"Kathy?"

"Yeah?"

"Thanks."

"Anytime. I'm glad you called me. I've missed you."

"I missed you guys too."

* * *

The protection spell called for Holly to create incense to spread throughout the house. The smell was ripe and smokey, and she wasn't sure how she'd be able to sleep if it lasted. If the magic behind it didn't keep evil away, the rancid smell would.

As she paraded around the house with a smoking kettle, her doorbell rang.

Her senses were on full alert. She set the kettle down and peered through the curtain before she answered the door. It was her neighbor, Aurora.

"Hi!" Holly tried to sound cheerful and relaxed, but she wasn't sure if it was coming across the way she intended.

Aurora gave a tight smile. "Hi. I just wanted to check in to make sure you were okay." She became serious. "Is something burning?"

Holly waved her hand in the air. "I just blew out a few candles."

"Right, okay. Are you sure you're okay?"

"Yeah, why wouldn't I be?"

"Well, I saw a man crash through your window today and he looked...distraught."

Holly couldn't keep her mouth from falling open. "Oh, you saw that?"

Aurora nodded. "Mmmm. And I just got this *feeling* that something was wrong over here. Like you were in a great deal of stress. Do you need to talk about anything?"

"Aurora, I promise you: everything is fine."

"Just a warning, Miss Holly, we don't condone lying. If anything like this happens again, the board will likely evict you."

Holly nodded. "I understand."

After Aurora left, Holly finished protecting the house. The possibility of eviction didn't bother her after the day she had had. She was moving back to Erie—a scary thought in itself.

Still, the idea that the neighbors had taken notice of Zamball's presence was unnerving. She didn't want to be watched constantly. For now, the best she could do was close all the curtains and turn off the lights. She lit a few scented candles to try to correct the awful smell of the incense and sat down with a pen and paper to write down a list of things she needed to do to move.

Getting out of the Assembly would make the moving process both easier and more difficult. She didn't personally own her house, the Assembly did, so she wouldn't have to worry about a mortgage.

Convincing the Board of Directors to let her go would be the trick. Although she kept to herself, she had regular customers who came during both the busy season and the slow season to see her. Severing those connections would be difficult to explain to the board, but she didn't want to use magic to sway their minds. They were all too keen on when something supernatural was happening. She had figured that out when she'd first arrived.

Holly was halfway through her list when she heard a rattling noise outside. She couldn't place where it was coming from. It was everywhere, really. She went to the window and pulled back the curtain. She couldn't believe what she was seeing.

In the middle of November, it was raining. Pouring, really. A second later, a clap of thunder sounded. This was certainly supernatural. It was a message. She knew exactly who was sending it.

Zamball.

MORE BY THE AUTHOR

To find the rest of the books in the Under the Moon Series as well as
more books by the author, visit
davidnethbooks.com/books

* * *

Subscribe to his newsletter to be the first to know of new releases and
special deals!
davidnethbooks.com/newsletter

* * *

If you enjoyed the book, please consider leaving a review on
Goodreads or the retailer you bought it from. Reviews help potential
readers determine whether they'll enjoy a book, so any comments on
what you thought of the story would be very helpful!

About the Author

David Neth is the author of the Under the Moon Series. He lives in Batavia, NY, where he dreams of a successful publishing career and opening his own bookstore.

Follow the Author

www.davidnethbooks.com
www.facebook.com/davidnethbooks
www.twitter.com/davidnethbooks
www.instagram.com/dneth13